Can Nat Nap?

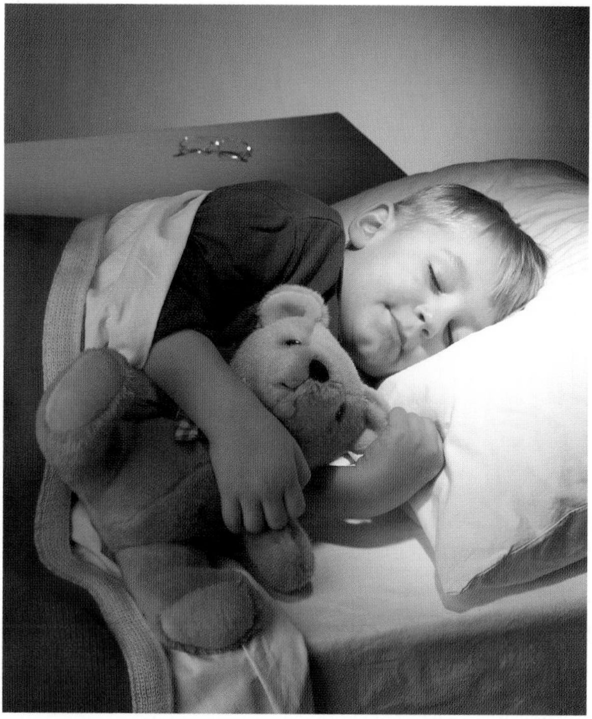

Written by Carol Hindin

Scott Foresman

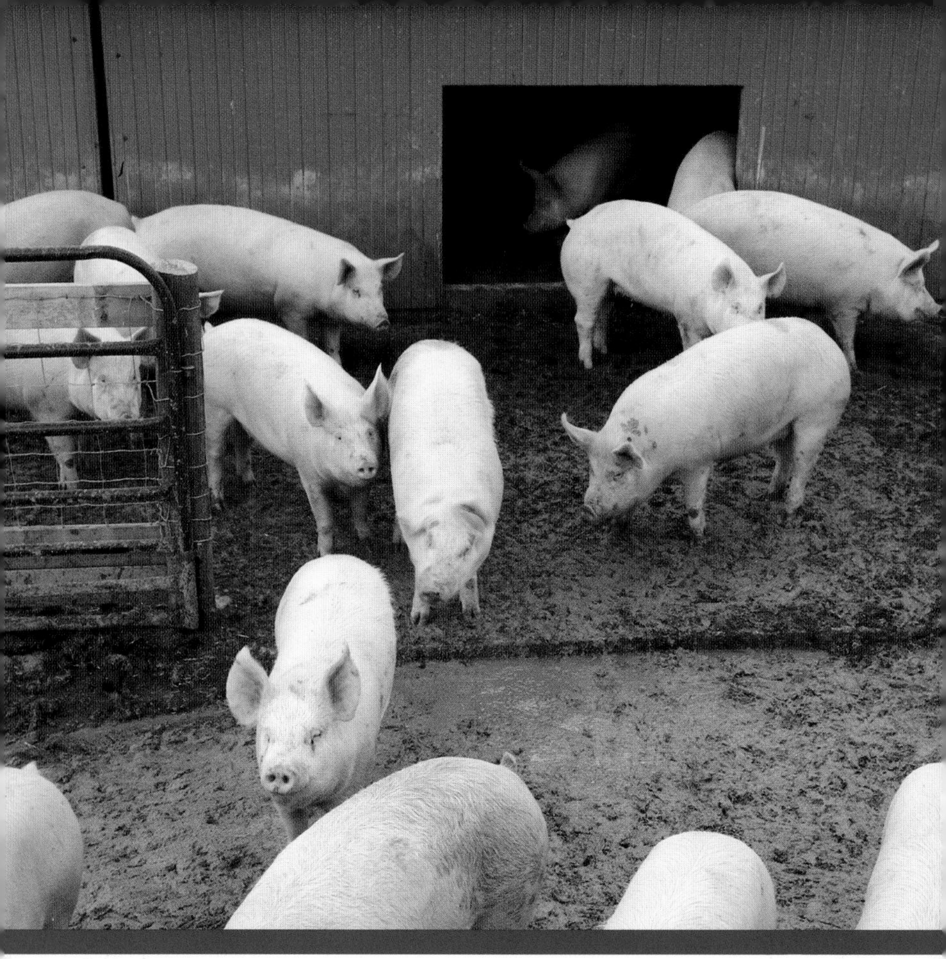

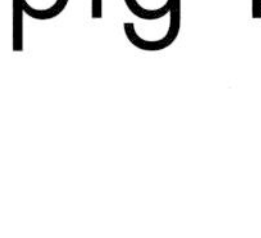

Is the pig big?

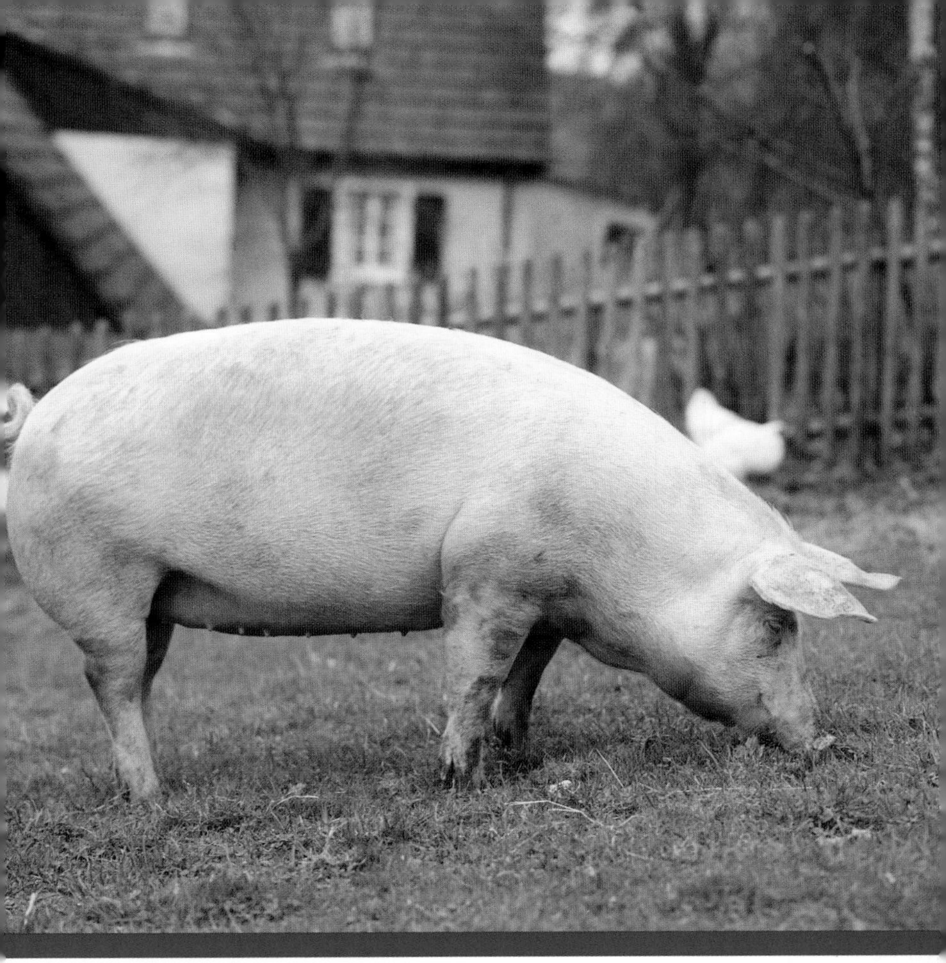

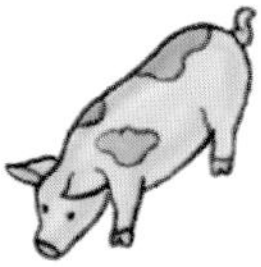

The pig is big.

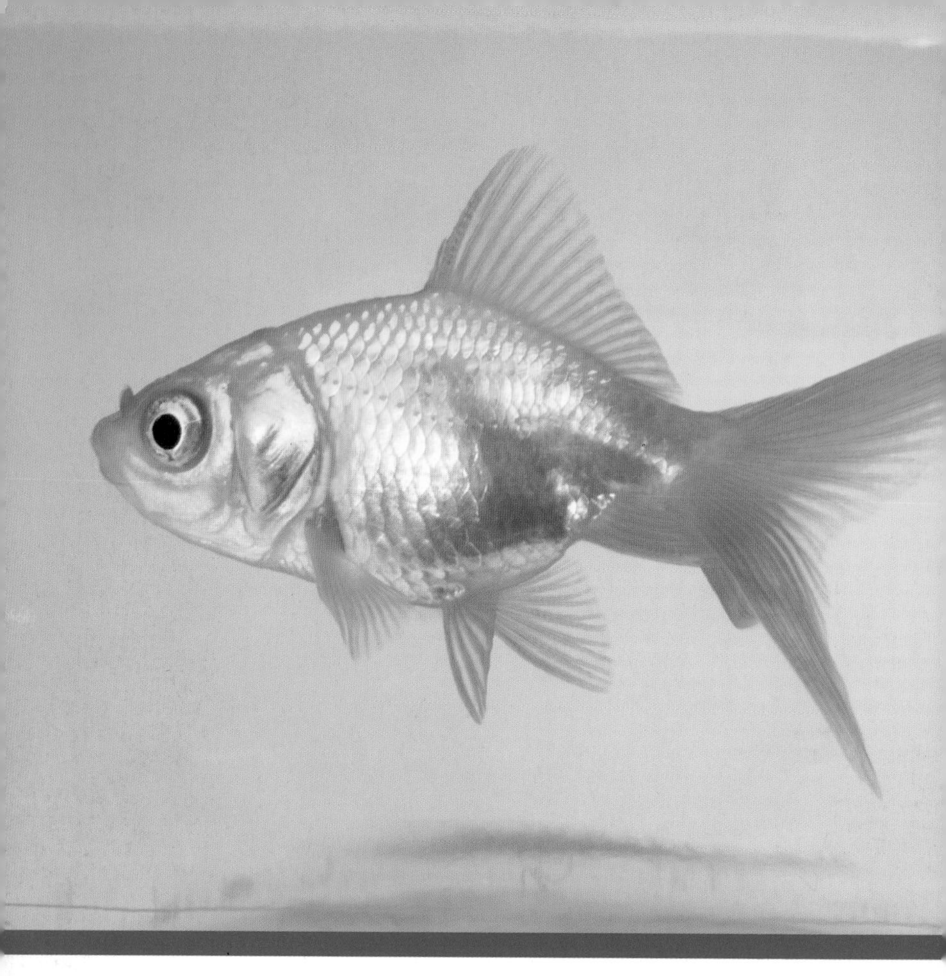

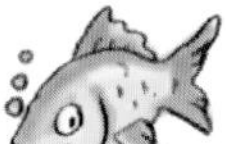

Is the fish in?

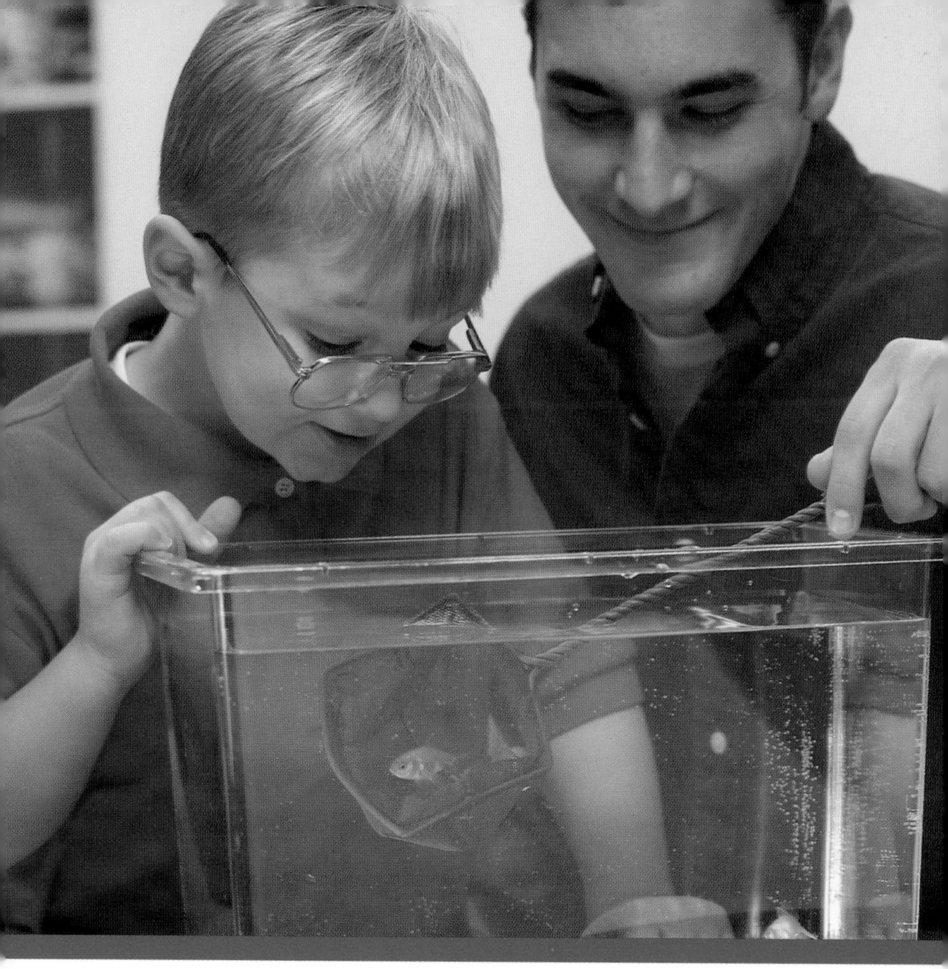

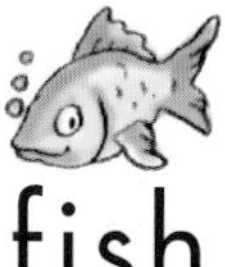

The fish is in.

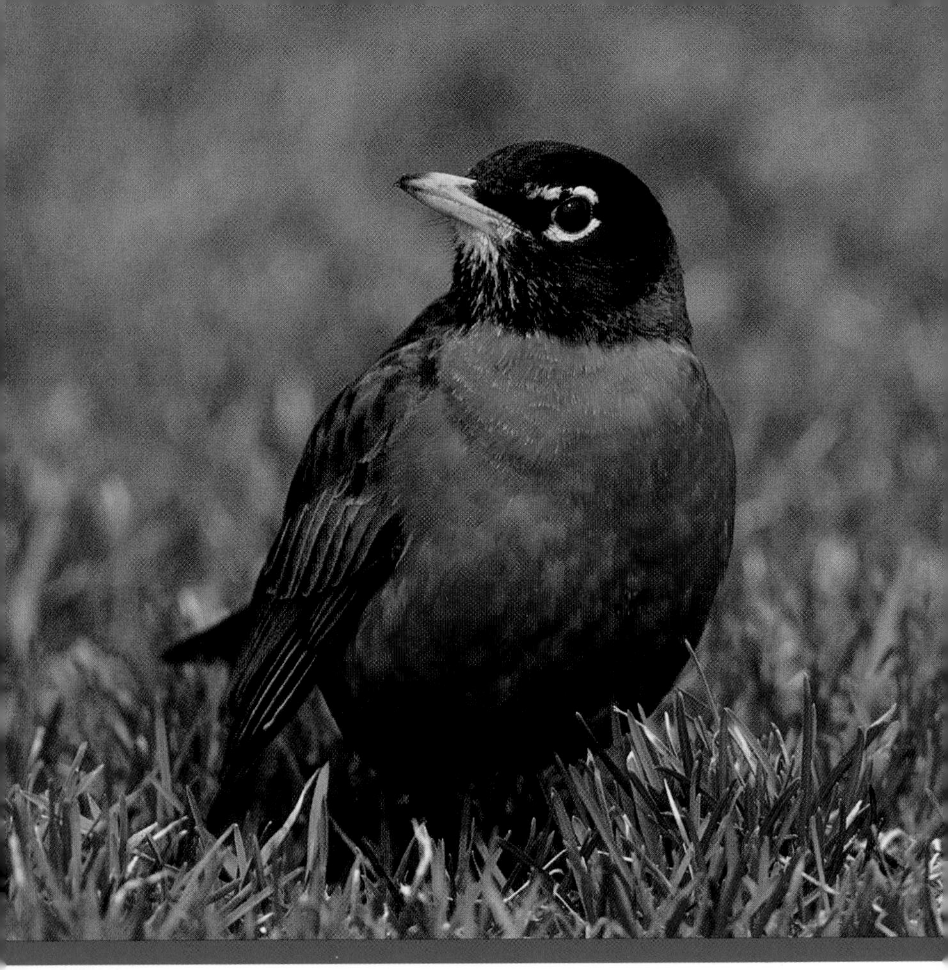

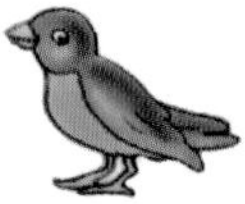

Can the bird nap?

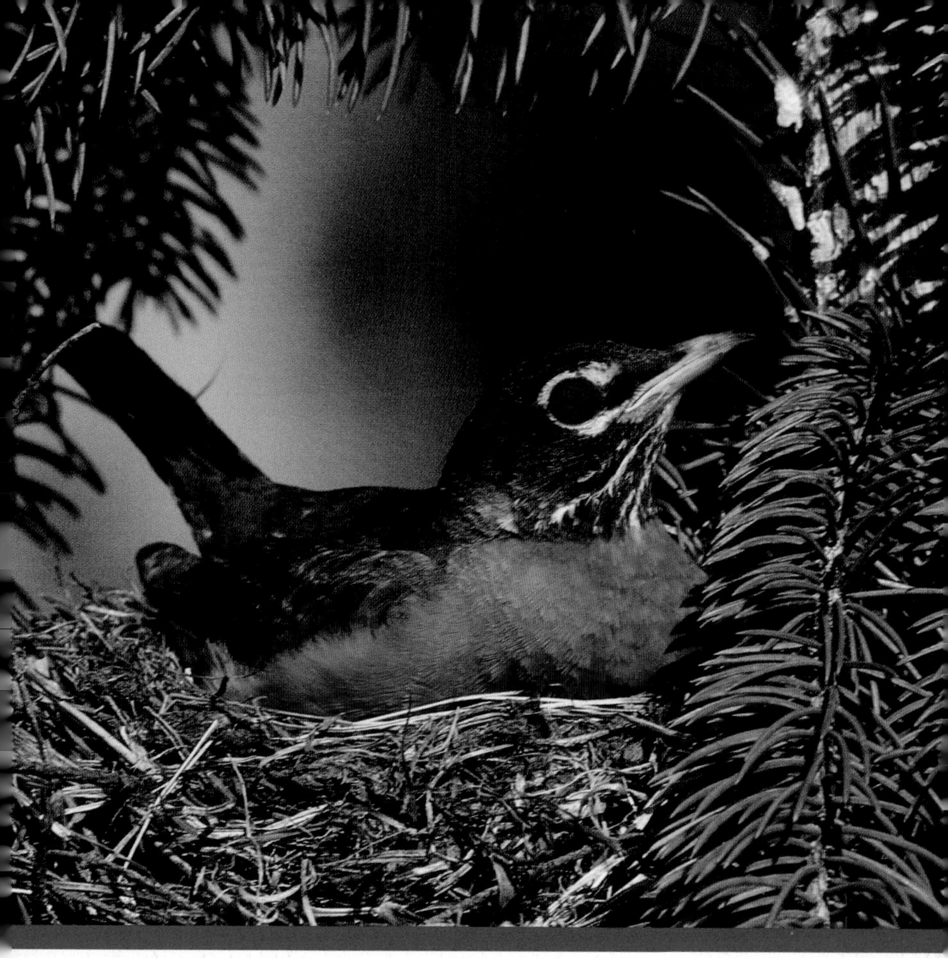

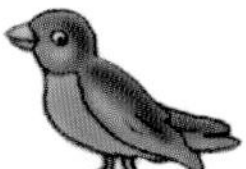

The bird can nap.

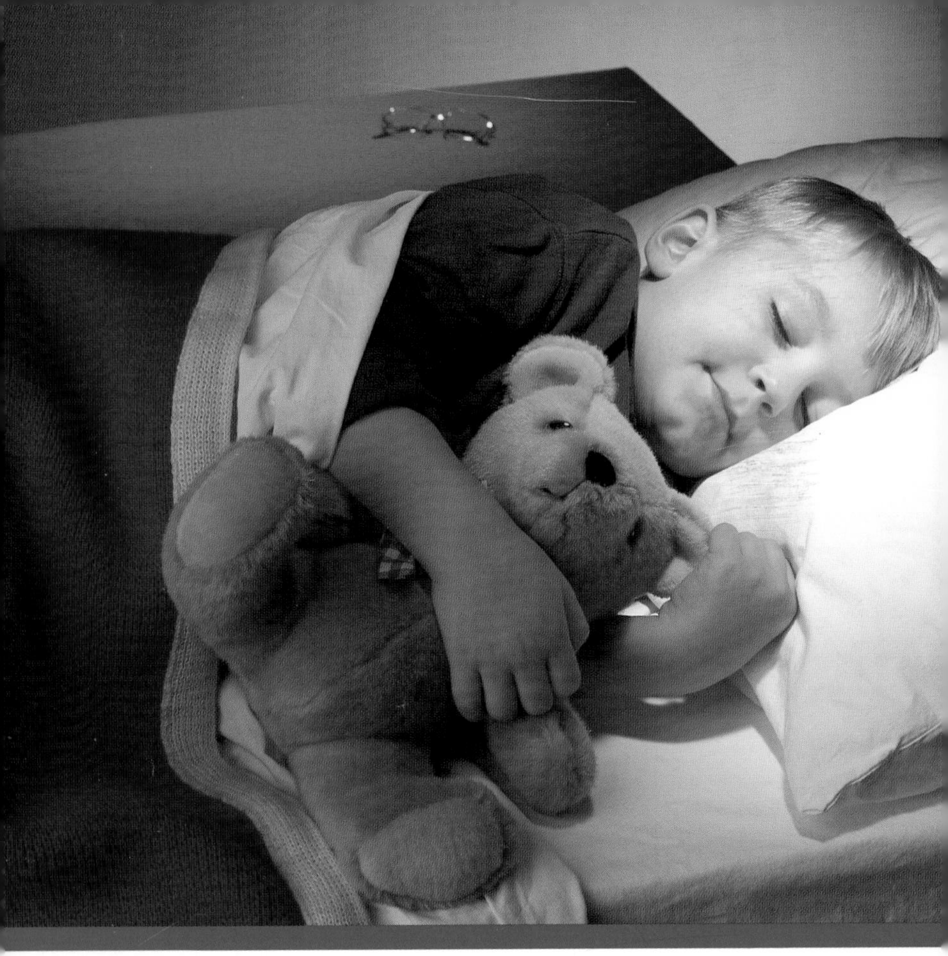

Like Nat.